For Mom and Dad

W1-Media, Inc.
Arctis Books USA
Stamford, CT, USA

Copyright © 2022 Haddy Jatou Njie and Lisa Aisato
First published by Cappelen Damm AS, 2016
Published in agreement with Oslo Literary Agency
First hardcover English edition published by W1-Media Inc. / Arctis USA 2022

Visit our website at www.arctis-books.com

1 3 5 7 9 8 6 4 2

The Library of Congress Control Number: 2021951732

ISBN 978-1-64690-023-7
English translation copyright © Megan Turney and Rachel Rankin

Cover design by Lisa Aisato
Printed in Latvia by Livonia Print, Riga, 2022.

FSC
www.fsc.org
MIX
Paper from
responsible sources
FSC® C002795

Haddy Njie and Lisa Aisato

A Dream for Every Season

Translated from the Norwegian by Megan Turney and Rachel Rankin

Arctis

Spring sleeps beneath a cozy quilt of freshly fallen snow.
With every breath, he reawakens all that lives and grows.

The ground above is frozen after months of wintry weather,
but he is warmed by pussy willow, lulled by downy feathers.

Now he dreams of ants and worms emerging from the gloom,
of butterflies unfurling wings, of buds becoming blooms.

Of flower after flower being combed by hungry bees,
of trickling from thawing streams, of bike pumps and pale knees.

Spring will soon awaken. Look—he stretches wild and free,
then skips in splits from roof to roof while bluebells ring with glee!

Spring comes after Winter's turn
while Summer stays in bed.
This is how it's always been—
now time to rest your head.

In springtime, Summer slumbers in a bud, a velvet bed,
with a cobweb full of treasures as a pillow for her head:

beads of amber, juicy berries, sand, and ocean spray,
sparkling drops of sticky honey, strands of golden hay.

She dreams of blossoming
beneath the sun's majestic eye,
of being nipped by gnats and
watching ladybugs fly by.

Of tender kisses, thunderclaps,
clean clothes, and daisy chains,
of barefoot walks on coastal rocks
and dancing pollen grains.

What do you notice about what summer is dreaming about?

Soon Summer will awaken. Look—she swings toward the skies
in a flourishing of blossoms, on the wings of butterflies!

Summer follows on from Spring
while Fall stays warm in bed.
This is how it's always been—
now time to rest your head.

What is "Fall" sleeping in?

Why do you think the author drew that?

Fall snoozes in the warmth within an apple's sweet embrace,
a look of golden restfulness upon her sleeping face.

Her hair is like an evening sky where storms and silence dwell.
She hums a tune of shorter days and casts her sunset spell.

She dreams of shaking pearls of rain from damp and dewy trees,
of frosty grass and chanterelles and berries fit to squeeze.

Of silent birds on journeys south, of air so crystal clear,
of cozy woolly sweaters and the last wasp of the year.

Fall will soon awaken. Look—she glides across the town
while swinging her umbrella, painting leaves red, gold, and brown!

Fall comes after Summer's turn
while Winter stays in bed.
This is how it's always been—
now time to rest your head.

Winter sleeps among the leaves,
her smile so warm and kind.
It's almost time for her to hide
what Summer left behind.

Stick out your tongue to catch
the snowflakes falling from the sky.
Can you taste the morning frost
and yummy pecan pie?

She dreams of mugs of cocoa and of footprints in the snow,
of people skiing, having fun, their cheeks a rosy glow.

Of cheerful candles burning bright, of gifts and candy canes,
of children skating on the ice and frosty windowpanes.

Why do you think "Winter" is dressed like that?

Soon Winter will awaken, make the world all gray and white,
peek down at us and whisper, "keep each other warm tonight!"

Winter follows on from Fall
while Spring stays warm in bed.
This is how it's always been—
now time to rest your head.